Lenny the Crow

written by
Angela Halgrimson
illustrated by
Brian Barber

This Book Belongs to _____

For Blake and Jake, the most polite boys in the world.
Or, at least, that's what their mom and dad tell them.

— A.H.

For Wyatt and Aden, who continue to ask for things,
even when I give them blank stares.

— B.B.

ISBN 13: 978-1-59298-968-3

Library of Congress Catalog Number: 2013914154

Printed in Canada

First Printing: 2013

17   16   15   14   13   5   4   3   2   1

Cover and interior design by Brian Barber

Edited by Kellie Hultgren and Lily Coyle

BEAVER'S POND
PRESS

7108 Ohms Lane
Edina, MN 55439-2129
(952) 829-8818
www.BeaversPondPress.com

To order, visit www.BeaversPondBooks.com or call 1-800-901-3480. Reseller discounts available.

This is Lenny. Lenny is a very **smart** crow.
At least, that is what his mother, Lucy, tells
him. Lenny is also the most **polite** crow.
That is what his father, Lyle, tells him.

One day when winter was near, Lenny and his family were searching for food and they met a raccoon in the woods.

Lucy said, "Excuse me, where can we find some food?"

Lyle added, "We haven't found enough to eat, and we're very hungry."

"You should meet the farmer who lives on the hill," said the raccoon. "He likes to feed animals! Every day he brings the horses and cows their food and even gives them fresh water to drink."

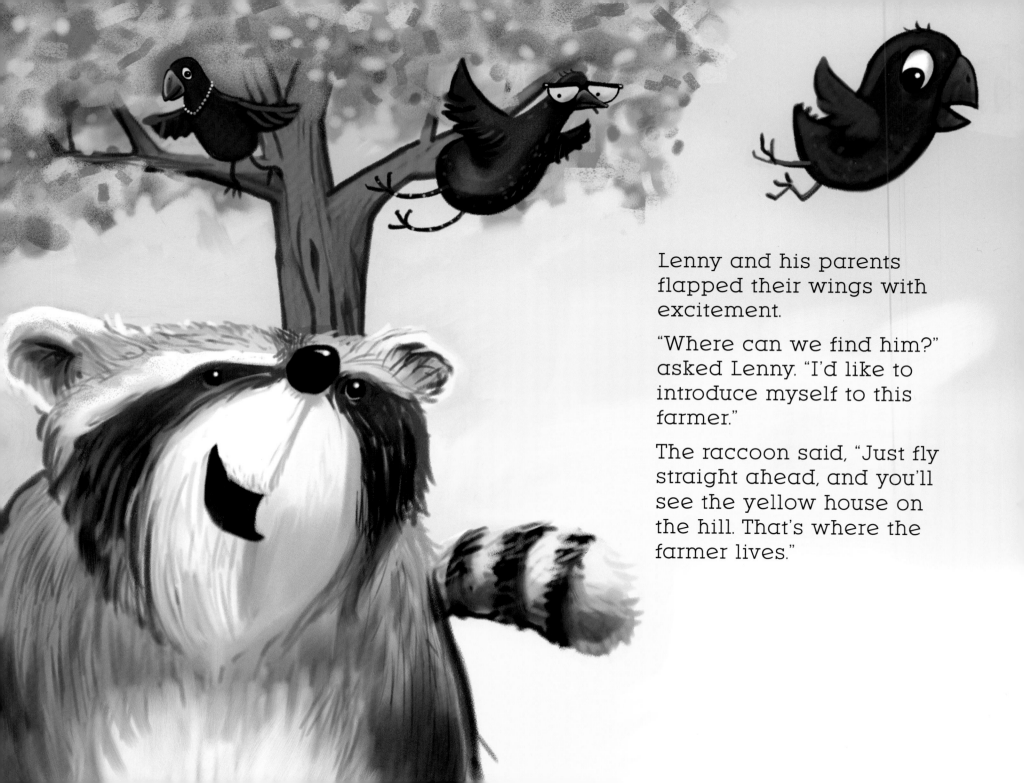

Lenny and his parents flapped their wings with excitement.

"Where can we find him?" asked Lenny. "I'd like to introduce myself to this farmer."

The raccoon said, "Just fly straight ahead, and you'll see the yellow house on the hill. That's where the farmer lives."

As the crow family flew toward the farm, Lenny had a worrying thought. *Birds have wings, not hands. How could he politely shake the farmer's hand?*

Well, he thought. *I'll just have to use my manners. The farmer will be happy to share with such well-behaved crows.*

As they flew over a field,
Lenny saw something below.

"Mom, Dad," he said,
"May I go look at that
green shiny thing?"

"Sure," his dad said.
"But don't get lost!"

Lenny was just about to land
when the farmer appeared—
right in front of him!

Lenny said, in his
most polite way,
"Hello, Mr. Farmer.
My name is Lenny!"

The farmer smiled,
but he did not say
anything back.

"Excuse me, Mr. Farmer," Lenny asked, "will you please give me some food? Winter is coming, and my family is very hungry."

The farmer just kept smiling.

This is odd, Lenny thought. *Maybe Mr. Farmer can't hear me. He's holding his hand out. He must want me to come closer.*

Lenny flew to the farmer's hand and raised his voice a little.

"Is this better?" he asked. **"Can you hear me now?"**

The farmer said nothing.

"Please, can we get some food from you, Mr. Farmer?"

Lenny almost shouted.

Again, the farmer said nothing.

Perhaps his hat is blocking his ears, Lenny thought.

He removed the farmer's hat and it fell to the ground.

Oops! Lenny thought. *That was a bit rude.*
But now he'll be able to hear me.

**"Hey, Mr. Farmer, I need to get some food.
Can you please bring some food to me?"**

Still, the farmer said nothing.

"please!"

Lenny cawed.

The farmer just stared straight ahead.

Mr. Farmer has very bad manners! Lenny thought. And even though he knew it wasn't nice, Lenny poked the farmer on the hand. The farmer did not move! Lenny poked the farmer on the arm—not **once**, but **twice**—and the farmer still didn't say anything.

"Caaaawwwww!"

Lenny yelled.

"What is wrong with you, farmer?"

Lenny just couldn't be polite any longer. He pecked a shiny button right off the farmer's shirt. And the farmer just smiled!

Lenny's anger grew with every button.

One...two...three...four...five...

Soon all the buttons were gone!

"Answer me, farmer!"
Lenny screamed.

Lenny snapped at the handkerchief
around the farmer's neck, and with
all his might, he yanked and pulled
on it. He was so out of control that
he didn't see his parents coming.

Animals came from everywhere to see why Lenny was yelling and screaming. They watched him yank and pull so hard that the stick the farmer was standing on began to wiggle in the ground.

"**Lenny!**" yelled his mom. "**What are you doing to that scarecrow?**"

"**Where did your manners go, Lenny?**" scolded his dad. "**The farmer has kindly put out food for all of the animals, and this is how you thank him?**"

Lenny saw all the animals staring at him.

Oh no! Lenny thought. *This scarecrow is* **not** *the farmer. Now everyone will laugh at me!* Lenny put his head down and didn't say anything.

Just then, the raccoon said, "What a brave young bird! I thought all crows were afraid of scarecrows!"

"Yes, very brave!"

"What a fearless young crow!" the other animals agreed. Lenny's mom and dad smiled.

Lenny looked up, and the raccoon winked at him.

From that day on, Lenny was not known as the **smartest** crow or even the most **polite** crow, but everybody knew that he was the **bravest** crow.

Or, at least, that's what his mom and dad told him.

The End.